The
Scared Ghost
and
Other
Stories

The Scared Ghost and Other Stories

retold by
Barbara Walker

McGraw-Hill Book Company

New York   St. Louis   San Francisco   Montreal   Toronto

Book design by Paulette Nenner

Library of Congress Cataloging in Publication Data
Walker, Barbara.
    The scared ghost, and other stories.
    CONTENTS: Middleton, R. On the road.—Hearn, L.
The boy who drew cats.—O'Sullivan, V. The interval.—
Stowe, H. B. The ghost in the mill. [etc.]
    1. Ghost stories.   2. Horror tales.
[1. Ghost stories.   2. Horror stories] I. Title.
PZ5.W152Sc   [Fic]   75-10950
ISBN 0-07-067812-X

123456789   BPBP   7898765

Contents

For My Family

The
Scared Ghost
and
Other
Stories

On the Brighton Road

by Richard Middleton

A cold wind swept across the level fields blowing fine dust of snow from the trees. As the morning sun rose higher and higher in the sky, a snow-covered mound by the side of a white road stirred. It was a tramp, struggling with the snow that had covered him during the night. He tossed like a person who awakens uncomfortably tangled in the sheet and blanket. Rising slowly to his feet, the tramp shook the snow from his clothes. As he did so the wind set him shivering, and he knew that his bed had been warm.

"Better get on down this road," he thought. "I'm only twelve miles from Brighton."

The snow-covered highway stretched before him into the distance as far as his eyes could see.

After about three miles he overtook a boy sitting by the side of the road. The lad wore no overcoat and looked tired and ill.

"Are you on the road?" The boy's voice was thick and husky with a bad cold.

"I think I am," the tramp said.

"Then I'll come a bit of the way with you if you don't walk too fast. It's a bit lonesome walking this time of day."

The tramp nodded his head "Yes," and the boy started limping along by his side.

"I'm fifteen," the boy said. "I bet you thought I was younger."

"Twelve, I'd have guessed," the tramp answered.

"Fifteen last August, and I've been on the road six years already. I ran away from home five times when I was little and the police took me back each time. Very good to me, the police were. Now I haven't got a home to run away from."

"Nor have I," the tramp said calmly.

"Oh, I can see what you are." The boy panted to keep up with the tramp's fast walking pace. "You're a gentleman come down low to a tramp. It's harder out here on the road for you than for me."

The tramp gazed at the limping, feeble boy and walked slower so that he could keep up. "I haven't been walking as long as you have," he admitted.

"No, I could tell that by the way you walk." The boy coughed and spit thick, yellow phlegm. "You haven't got tired yet."

"Tired! Only the Devil knows how many miles I walked yesterday, maybe forty. I was so tired last night I dropped by the roadside and slept where I fell. Freezing cold and snowing like it was, it's a wonder I didn't die."

On the Brighton Road

The boy looked at him sharply. "How do you know you didn't?"

"What are you talking about, boy!" The tramp was angry. He didn't have the mind to bother with crazy boys talking foolishness.

"Do you think I'm not dead?" The boy grabbed the tramp's arm. His grip was hard and firm in spite of his weak, feeble appearance. "I was drowned bathing at Margate. Another time I was killed by a man with a spike. He bashed my head in. Twice I froze to death like you did last night."

The tramp snatched his arm away. Still the boy persisted. He would not give up. "A motor car cut me down on this very road. Yet I'm walking along here now, walking to Brighton to walk away from it again. I can't help it. I tell you we can't get away, even if we want to. *We're dead!*" The boy broke off in a fit of coughing.

"You'd better borrow my coat a bit, lad." The tramp laid his hand gently on the boy's shoulder.

"Don't touch me!" His voice was fierce. "I don't want your coat. I'm all right. I was telling you about the road. We're all dead. You don't know it yet, but you'll find out."

Suddenly the boy lurched forward. The tramp caught him in his arms.

"I'm sick," he whispered "—sick."

The tramp looked up and down the road, but

could see no houses or any sign of help. Yet, even as he supported the boy doubtfully in the middle of the road, a black motor car appeared on the horizon. It came quietly on out of the white stillness of the snow. Its engine purring softly.

"What's the trouble?" The driver got out and kneeled in the snow beside the shivering boy. "I'm a doctor." He looked at the boy and listened to his strained breathing. "Pneumonia," he announced. "I'll take him to the hospital and give you a lift, too, if you'd like."

The tramp shook his head. "I'd rather walk."

The tramp looked into the boy's pale face as he helped the doctor lift him into the car. Dark-blue circles surrounded his sunken eyes. He was very ill. Before the doctor closed the door, the boy clutched the tramp's hand. "I'll meet you beyond Brighton," he muttered. "You'll see."

"That's right, son." The tramp didn't often lie. But he thought this one time wouldn't hurt him none on the Judgment Day. Why should he fuss with a dying boy?

All the morning the tramp splashed through the thawing snow. At noon he begged some bread at a cottage door and crept into a lonely barn to eat it. A black-and-white-spotted milk cow kept him company. It was warm in the barn and after his meager meal he fell asleep on a bed of straw. The sky was dark when he woke and started trudging once more down the slushy road.

Two miles beyond Brighton a man called to him from the darkness by the side of the road.

"On the road?" the voice asked.

"I think I am," the tramp replied.

"Then I'll come a bit of the way with you if you don't walk too fast. It's a bit lonesome walking this time of day."

A slim, limping figure stepped into the road. The tramp cried out in horror when he saw the boy—"But the pneumonia!" he screamed.

"I died at Brighton this morning," said the boy, smiling.

The Boy Who Drew Cats

by Lafcadio Hearn

A long time ago in a small country village in Japan, there lived a poor farmer, his wife, and their children. Everyone in the family worked very hard. When the oldest son was only ten years old he helped his father in the fields. The little girls learned to help their mother with chores almost as soon as they could walk. Later, when the girls grew older they stood ankle-deep in the muddy water of the rice fields, helping their mother plant the tender young rice shoots.

The youngest child, a little boy, did not seem fit for hard farm work. Although he was cleverer than all his brothers and sisters, he was quite weak and small. People said he could never grow very big. This worried the poor farmer and his wife. What would become of their son if he did not grow strong enough to become a farmer?

One day the farmer and his wife took their little son with them to the village temple. They asked the priest to take the boy as his pupil and teach him all that a priest should know.

The old priest spoke kindly to the lad, and asked him some hard questions. The boy's answers were so clever that the priest agreed to take him into the temple. The farmer and his wife went away happy. Their problem was solved. Their son would become a priest.

The boy learned everything that the old priest taught him. But he had one fault. He liked to draw cats during study hours, and to draw cats when cats ought not to have been drawn at all. Whenever he found himself alone, he drew cats. He drew them on the margins of the priest's books, on all the paper screens in the temple, and on the walls. Several times the priest told him this was not right. Still the boy did not stop drawing cats.

One day the priest caught him drawing some very clever pictures of cats on a paper screen. The old priest was upset that the boy continued to be disobedient. There was only one thing to do. "My boy," the priest said, "you must go away from this temple at once. You will never make a good priest, but perhaps you will become a great artist. Now let me give you a last piece of advice. Be sure you never forget it: *Avoid large places at night; keep to small!*"

The boy did not know what the priest meant by saying, *"Avoid large places; keep to small!"* He thought and thought, while he was tying up his little bundle of clothes to go away. He could not understand those words, but he was afraid to speak to the priest, except to say good-bye.

He left the temple very sorrowfully, and

began to wonder what he should do. He was afraid to go home. He felt certain that his father would punish him for being an artist when he should have been studying to become a priest. All at once he remembered that a village a few miles away had a very big temple with several priests. He made up his mind to go there and ask to become a pupil.

Now that big temple was closed up, but the boy did not know this. The reason it had been closed was that a goblin had frightened the priests away, and had taken over the place. Some brave warriors had gone to the temple at night to kill the goblin. They had never been seen alive again. Nobody had ever told these things to the boy. He walked all the way to the village, hoping to be kindly treated by the priests.

When he got to the village it was already dark. All the people were in bed. At the end of the main street he saw a light in the temple. People who tell the story say the goblin used the light to tempt lonely travelers to ask for shelter. The boy went at once to the temple and knocked. There was no sound from inside. He knocked and knocked again. Still nobody came. At last he pushed gently at the door. It was not locked. He went in and saw a lamp burning brightly, but no priests.

The boy thought that someone would be sure to come very soon, so he sat down to wait. He noticed that everything in the temple was gray with dust, and thickly spun over with cobwebs. These priests, he thought, would certainly be happy to have a pupil who could keep the temple clean. The boy looked around the room. The dust was a great puzzle to him. But it was quickly forgotten when he noticed several big white folding paper screens standing in a corner. What harm, he thought, in painting a few cats? Surely, they would make the plain screens much more beautiful.

After he had painted a great many cats on the screens, the boy began to feel sleepy. He was just about to rest his head on the floor to sleep when he remembered the warning—*"Avoid large places at night; keep to small!"*

The temple was very large. As he thought of the words, the boy began to feel a little afraid. He decided to search for a small place to sleep. At last he found a little cabinet with a sliding door. He crawled inside and shut himself up. He lay on his side with his knees drawn up to his chin and fell fast asleep.

Very late in the night he was awakened by a most terrible noise—a noise of fighting and screaming. It was so dreadful that he was afraid even to look through a crack in the little cabinet door. He lay very still, holding his breath from fright.

The light that had been in the temple went out, but the awful sounds continued. If anything, they grew more terrible in the darkness. All the temple shook. After a long time, silence came. Still the boy was afraid to move. He did not move until the light of the morning sun shone into the cabinet through the crack in the door.

He climbed out of his hiding place very cautiously and looked about. The first thing he saw was that all the temple floor was covered with blood. And then he saw lying dead in the middle of the floor an enormous rat—bigger than a cow. It was a goblin rat!

But who or what could have killed it? His eyes scanned the room. When the boy saw the screens a terrible cry burst from his lips and echoed in the empty temple. The mouths of all the cats he had drawn were red and wet with blood.

With the passing of time, the boy became a man and the man became a great artist. Even today, travelers in Japan can see some of his pictures of cats.

The Interval

by Vincent O'Sullivan

Mrs. Wilton walked slowly along the wide, quiet street looking anxiously from one side to the other searching for the small antique shop. She pulled up the wide collar on her coat to cover her ears. After living in India she found the London climate cold and damp. Today the fog hung close to the ground. She felt that she was walking through clouds—wet clouds that covered her hair and coat with tiny drops of moisture.

She paused before the door of a tiny antique shop and peered through the dirty window. Inside she saw used furniture and a carelessly arranged display of jewelry in a glass case. She stepped back and read the name printed in white letters on the glass pane—FINEGOLD.

A bell answered her entrance with an ill-tempered jangle. From somewhere in the back of the shop the antique dealer came forward. He had a white face, with a spare black beard, and spectacles. Mrs. Wilton spoke to him in a low voice, asking to see the woman.

"Yes, she is here, madam," he answered. "Whether she will see you or not I don't know. She has her moods."

The Scared Ghost and Other Stories

Mrs. Wilton followed him to the back of the shop to a winding staircase. At the foot of the stairs he lit a candle.

"You must go up these steps. It's very dark —be careful. At the top you will see a door. Open it and go straight in."

He stood at the foot of the stairs, holding the light high above his head as she climbed.

The room that she entered was not very large, and it seemed very ordinary. There were some flimsy, uncomfortable chairs in gilt and red. She saw pictures of children under a glass cover on a table. Mrs. Wilton thought that the room did not look like a place of business. There was no suggestion that this was a waiting room where people came and went all day. At the same time, it did not look like a private room that someone lived in. There were no books or papers about. There was no fire and it was very cold.

The other door to the room was covered with a heavy black velvet curtain. Mrs. Wilton pulled a chair from under a table in the center of the room and sat down. She watched the door with the velvet curtain, certain that the soothsayer would come through it. This must be the tenth seer she had seen, trying to find someone to help her speak with her dead husband, Hugh.

She thought about the others who had said they could help her. No, this was the eleventh. She had almost forgotten about that frightening man in Paris who said he had been a priest. Of all the others she had seen, only he had told her anything definite. But he could do no more than tell her about the past. He told her of her marriage to Hugh. He knew they had been married only two years before he died. He even knew that Hugh had been a soldier and that they went to India to live because he was stationed there.

Mrs. Wilton was so lost in her thoughts she did not hear the woman enter the room and sit at the table. She was startled to see her. She was even more surprised by the woman's appearance. There was nothing about her to suggest that she could communicate with the dead. The woman obviously was a seamstress, for her plain black dress was covered with bits of thread. A fat little woman, she breathed heavily and had a nervous habit of rubbing her hands together. She wet her lips with her tongue and barked a hoarse, dry cough. Mrs. Wilton thought sadly that the woman had spent too many years of her life bent over a sewing machine making dresses she was too poor to wear. Bits of thread had even got into her hair. Her skin was smooth. She had once been pretty.

"I want to explain—" Mrs. Wilton began, then hesitated. The woman was staring beyond her at the wall.

"Can't you see him? He is so near." The words came thick and heavy and slow from the woman's mouth. "He is passing his arm around your shoulders."

At that moment, Mrs. Wilton did indeed feel someone very near. She knew that only a thin veil prevented her from seeing her darling husband. But the woman saw him. She described Hugh in every detail, including the burn on his right hand. Mrs. Wilton was overcome. She had searched so long for someone to help her talk with Hugh. Now she didn't know what to say. She could only stammer the first thing that came into her head.

"Is he happy? Oh, ask him, does he love me?"

"He loves you. He won't answer, but he loves you. He wants me to make you see him. He is disappointed that I cannot. You must do it yourself."

After a while she said, "I think you will see him again. You think of nothing else. He is very close to us now."

Without warning, the woman collapsed onto the table and lay motionless in a heavy sleep. Mrs. Wilton put some money on the table and stole out of the room on tiptoe.

Mrs. Wilton's mind was in a fog as thick as that covering the London streets. She seemed to remember that downstairs the man tried to sell her some old silver jewelry, but she did not regain her senses 'till she realized that she was entering an old church.

The church was dimly lit and empty. Mrs.

The Interval

Wilton sat on one of the polished black pews and bent forward with her face in her hands, weeping. Was Hugh truly separated from her forever?

After a few minutes she heard someone enter. A soldier walked down the aisle and sat about six rows ahead of her. First she thought that he looked a little like her Hugh. Then he turned to her and raised his hand; it was Hugh!

"Oh, my darling you have come back." She hurried toward him. "You are not dead, it was all a mistake."

Suddenly footsteps echoed behind her and a voice called out. She turned to see who approached.

"I thought I heard you call," the old man who cleaned the church said.

"I was talking with my husband," she said excitedly.

But Hugh was nowhere to be seen.

It might have been two or three days after that when she saw him again. She sat in a little restaurant where they used to eat together. She had arrived late and was the only customer. Hunger had driven her there; now she nibbled at the food—her appetite gone and loneliness returned. She could almost have cried from the ache in her heart. Then suddenly Hugh was sitting opposite her at the table. Just like old times, he smiled at her and urged her to eat.

The
Scared Ghost
and
Other
Stories

She found that by going to places where she had once seen him, the church or the restaurant, she was likely to see him again. She never saw him at her apartment. But in the street or in the park he would often walk beside her. Once he saved her from being run over. She felt his hand pushing her to safety when the car was nearly upon her.

Mrs. Wilton lived in solitude, almost completely alone, seeing only those people who took the trouble to visit her. To friends who were worried about her strange talk of Hugh and about her health, she laughed and said she was very well—and so was Hugh.

One sunny morning she was lying in bed awake. The shy London sunlight peeped through the blinds, giving the room a fresh, cheerful look.

She heard the door open and thought it was the maid bringing tea. But when she looked up Hugh was standing at the foot of the bed. Dressed in his military uniform, he looked as he had the day he went away.

He smiled and threw back his head, just as he did in the old days at her mother's house. It was his way of calling her from the room without attracting attention from the others. He picked up her little red slippers and signaled for her to put them on and follow. She slipped out of bed hastily. . . .

The Interval

The maid found her that morning, dead. Her friends thought it strange when they came to pack her belongings to give them away to a charity—her red slippers could not be found.

The Ghost in the Mill

by Harriet Beecher Stowe

We boys had made plans for a comfortable evening, having enticed Sam Lawson— well known as the best storyteller south of Boston—to the chimney corner. We had drawn him a mug of cider and set down a row of apples to roast on the hearth. Even now they were giving faint sighs and sputters as their plump sides burst from the heat. The big oak log in the fireplace snapped and popped, dropping a shower of sparks amid the ashes. The whole area of the chimney was full of a sleepy warmth and brightness, just right for one of Sam Lawson's stories. Sam tilted his head far back, emptied the mug of cider down his scrawny throat, then began—

"There used to be a fellow come around these parts, spring and fall, peddling goods from a pack on his back. He was named Jehiel Lommedieu. Nobody knew where he came from. He wasn't much of a talker and never said. Anyway, the women folks liked him. He got to be so popular with them that they would keep track of the weeks that he was away peddling in other parts of Massachusetts. They'd figure out when he would be around our way again, then they'd go making gingersnaps and preserves and pies for him. When he showed up they'd make him stay to teas at their houses and feed him on the best they had. He never seemed to mind the teas, and it kept the women happy. Their husbands weren't jealous of this fellow because he was skinny and not much to look at.

"A story started going around that he was courting Phoebe Ann Parker—more than likely she had set her cap for him. Well, all of a sudden, Lommedieu stopped coming around and nobody knew why. Least of all, Phoebe Ann, because she had a letter from him that said he would be in the area at Thanksgiving time. He didn't come at Thanksgiving. Christmas came and went and still no Lommedieu.

"In the spring, Phoebe Ann got tired of waiting and married somebody else. By the fall, pretty much everybody had given up looking for him. Some said he was dead, killed by Indians. Some said he had gone up to Canada. A few even said he had gone back to England. For certain, Lommedieu was gone from people's thoughts by the time he turned up again—in a most unexpected place.

"Captain Ed Sawin told me this story about Lommedieu and I take it for the gospel truth, because Captain Ed is a very respectable man, a deacon in the church.

"Captain Ed set out to haul a load of lumber

The Ghost in the Mill

to Boston. That day there came the biggest sudden snowstorm that had been seen in these parts for as long as anybody could remember. The captain used to say that he could stand any wind that blew from one direction, but this wind blew from every direction and kicked up snow in such swirls that he could hardly see the road in front of the horses. The captain figured the animals would keep to the track. But after he had gone along a spell, he realized that the horses were as blinded by the snow as he was. They had strayed from the Boston road and he was lost. He kept going the wrong way 'cause it wasn't wise to stop in the middle of a blizzard, especially when it was coming on nightfall and the temperature might drop to freezing. That was no time to be caught outside.

"Before it got too dark, the captain got his bearings and realized that he was near Crack Sparrock's mill. Crack was a dreadful, drinking old critter who lived alone in the woods attending to his grist mill. Folks saw him only when they took grain to be milled into flour. Time was when Crack was a decent fellow, but after his wife died he just turned his back on the world and got meaner every year.

"When the captain saw darkness coming on fast and the storm didn't seem to be letting up, he figured he's best go on up to Crack's house and ask for shelter. He unhitched his horses, didn't want to leave them outside in such weather, and struggled off through the snow to Crack Sparrock's mill.

"Captain Ed knocked at the door and got no answer. He knew Crack wouldn't be outside on a wild night, so he opened the door and went in. To be sure, Crack was home. There he sat beside a great blazing fire with his rum jug at his side.

"Captain Ed spoke right up. 'Crack, I'm off my road and got snowed down not far from here.'

"'Guess you'll just have to camp down here till morning.' Crack was very hospitable. He got dressed in his warm clothes and went outside to help Captain Ed put his horses into the shed so they would be warmer and out of the weather. By the time they got back inside the storm was roaring something awful. But Crack put more wood on his fire and put on the tea kettle and made a pot of hot toddy—with rum—to keep their spirits up. Soon he and the captain were having a good time drinking and laughing and telling tall tales. About midnight there came a loud rap on the door.

"'What's that?' Crack was startled, as it was a terrible blowy night and it was a little scary to have a caller so late.

"Captain Ed didn't feel much better about the rap at the door. They waited in silence for a minute. There was no sound except the screeching wind. Crack was just about to go on with his story when the rap came again—harder, this time.

"'If it's the Devil,' said Crack, walking to the door, 'we'd better let him in and have it out with him.'

"Captain Ed said he never saw a fellow as scared as Crack was when he saw Ketury standing at his door with not a footprint in the snow to show how she got there. You see, Ketury was an Indian and everybody knew she was a witch.

"Leaning on her walking stick, the woman shuffled into the cabin and sat on a chair near the fire. She was withered and wrinkled and brown, and her little black eyes snapped with sparks of gold. It kinda made your head dizzy to look at her eyes. Folks used to say that anybody Ketury got mad at was sure to get the worst end of the bargain. And so, no matter what hour of the day or night she had a mind to rap at anybody's door, folks thought it best to let her in. She was like the wind. She came when the fit was on her, stayed so long as it pleased her, and left when she got ready—not before.

"Ketury understood English and could speak it well enough, but she always seemed to scorn the language—and the people who spoke it.

"Crack poured her a cup of hot toddy, but her being there put a damper on the good time

The Scared Ghost and Other Stories

he and Captain Ed had been having. Besides, she sat rocking back and forth, sipping her toddy, muttering and looking up the chimney.

"Captain Ed said in all his born days he never heard such screeching and yells as the wind gave over that chimney. Old Crack, he said, got so frightened you could fairly hear his teeth chatter.

"Captain Ed wasn't going to have good conversation stopped by a woman, witch or no witch. And so when he saw Ketury muttering and looking up the chimney, he spoke up. 'Well, Ketury what do you see?' said he. 'Come on out with it. Don't keep it to yourself.' You see, the captain was feeling pretty courageous from all those rum toddies. Otherwise he never would have dared to speak to Ketury like that.

"Anyway, Ketury rattled her necklace of bear teeth (I don't know for sure what kind of teeth they were) and looked up the chimney and called out, 'Come down, come down, let's see who ye be.'

"Then there was a scratching and a rumbling and a groan, and a pair of feet came down the chimney and stood right in the middle of the hearth. The shoes on the feet had silver buckles a-shining in the firelight. Captain Ed says he never came so near to being scared in his life. As to old Crack, he just wilted right down in his chair.

"Then Ketury got up and reached her stick

up the chimney and called out louder, 'Come down, come down! Let's see who ye be.' Sure enough, down came a pair of legs and joined on to the feet—good straight legs they were, with ribbed stockings and leather breeches.

"'Well, we're in for it now,' said Captain Ed to Ketury. 'Let's have the rest of him.'

"Ketury didn't seem to mind Captain Ed. She stood there as still as a stake and kept calling out, 'Come down, come down! Let's see who ye be.' And then came down the body of a man with a brown coat and a yellow vest and joined right on the legs. But there wasn't no arms to the body. Ketury shook her stick up the chimney and called, *'Come down, come down!'* Out floated a pair of arms and went on each side of the body. There stood a man all finished, only there wasn't a head on him.

"Said Captain Ed, 'This is getting serious, Ketury. Finish him up and let's see what he wants of us.'

"Ketury called out once more, 'Come down, come down! Let's see who ye be.' A man's head came down the chimney and settled on the shoulders. The captain's eyes popped—Jehiel Lommedieu!

"Old Crack fell flat on his face on the floor and prayed to the Lord to have mercy on his soul. But Captain Ed was for getting to the bottom of matters. He said to Lommedieu, 'What do you want? Why have you come?'

"The ghost didn't speak, he only moaned and pointed up the chimney. Lommedieu seemed to try to speak, but couldn't, for you know it isn't often that ghosts are allowed to talk. Just then there came a screeching blast of wind that tore the door open and blew smoke and fire and ashes all into the room. There seemed to be a whirlwind inside the cabin—a whirlwind of darkness filled with moans and screeches. When it all cleared up, Ketury and Jehiel Lommedieu were both gone.

"Crack didn't live for but a day or two after that. He died before they could hang him for murdering the peddler for his money and stuffing his body up the chimney. After Crack died, they tore down the old mill, found the skeleton of Jehiel Lommedieu, and gave it a decent burial."

The Scared Ghost

Author Unknown

Once upon a time there was a poor barber who did not live happily with his wife.

"Why did you marry me," she complained, "if you did not have means to support a wife? When I was in my father's house I had plenty to eat, but it seems that I have come to your house to starve."

The barber's wife did not content herself with words. One day her anger over her husband's small earnings drove her to attack him with a broomstick.

Stung with shame on account of his wife's beating, the barber left his house, taking the tools of his craft—razors, whetstone for sharpening them, scissors, and mirror—and vowed not to return until he had become a rich man.

The barber traveled from village to village. Everywhere he found work, but nothing that would make him rich. Toward nightfall one day, he came to the outskirts of a forest and lay himself down at the foot of a tree. In that spot, he spent many sad hours feeling sorry for himself because of his hard lot in life.

It so chanced that this tree was the home of a ghost. The ghost, seeing a human being at the foot of his tree, became angry and thought only of destroying him. The ghost leaped from his tree with outspread arms and gaping mouth, and stood tall before the barber.

"Now I am going to destroy you!" he screeched. "Who will protect you and save your life?"

The barber, quaking in every limb from fear, his hair standing erect, did not lose his presence of mind. Shrewdly, he laughed at the ghost.

"You will destroy me! I'll show you the ghost I have captured this very night and put into my bag. Right glad I am to find you here, for you shall make one more ghost for my collection."

The barber reached into his bag, pulled out a small mirror, and held it up so that the ghost saw his own face.

"Here you see one ghost which I have already caught," said the barber. "I'm going to put you in the bag to keep this ghost company."

The ghost, seeing his own face in the mirror, was very frightened. "Oh, sir, please don't put me in your bag," he cried. "I will do whatever you bid me. I will give you whatever you want."

"You ghosts are a faithless lot," answered the barber. "You will promise and then not deliver."

"Oh, sir, take pity on me," pleaded the ghost. "Give me a chance to do your bidding. If I fail, then put me in your bag."

"Very well," said the barber. "First, you must bring me one thousand gold coins. Then, by tomorrow night, you must make a granary at my house and fill it with rice. Go now and get the gold immediately. If you fail, into the bag you go!"

The ghost gladly agreed to the conditions. He went away and quickly returned with a bag of gold.

The barber was delighted beyond measure at the sight of the gold coins. He ordered the ghost to see to it that the granary was built, and quickly too. "You only have one night to get the job done."

During the small hours of the morning, after midnight and before daybreak, the barber knocked at the door of his house. Now, his wife had spent many days and nights regretting that she struck her husband with her broomstick and caused him to leave his home. When she unbolted the door and saw him she was over-joyed, for since he had been gone she realized that she loved him dearly. Her husband told her of the ghost and poured a glittering heap of gold coins from his bag to prove that he spoke the truth.

The next night the fearful ghost raised a large granary at the barber's house and worked the livelong night carrying large bags of rice till he had filled the granary to the brim.

The uncle of this terrified ghost, seeing his nephew work so hard, asked what had happened to him. When he heard the story, the uncle-ghost laughed. "You fool," he said, "the barber is a cunning fellow. He has cheated you. He can't bag you!"

"If you doubt the barber's power," replied the nephew-ghost, "go and learn for yourself what he can do."

The uncle-ghost went to the barber's house, and peeped in through a window. The barber felt a blast of wind and knew it meant a ghost was near. He saw the uncle-ghost peering in at his window. Immediately he placed a mirror before the uncle's face.

"Aha!" the barber screamed, "a new ghost to put into my bag!"

The uncle-ghost was frightened out of his wits by the sight of his own face. He promised to raise a second granary at the barber's house that very night and fill it with corn if the barber would not put him into his bag. The bargain made, the ghost went away to begin his work.

And that is the way the barber became a rich man in corn, in rice, and in gold.

The Flying Dutchman

by Auguste Jal

Many years ago there lived a ship's captain who feared neither God nor all His saints. He was a Dutchman, it is said, but in what town he was born is not known nor does it matter. He sailed all the seven seas in every weather imaginable. It was his boast that no storm, however terrible, could make him turn back.

On one voyage to the Cape of Good Hope, he ran into a headwind that might have blown the horns off an ox. What with the wind and the huge waves the ship was in great danger. Everyone aboard urged the captain to turn back.

"We are lost if you don't turn back, Captain!" they pleaded. "If you keep trying to round the Cape in this wind, we shall sink."

The captain only laughed at the fears of his passengers and crew. Instead of heeding them he broke into songs so vile that just by themselves they might have drawn the lightning to strike the masts of the ship. Then he called for his pipe and his tankard of beer. He smoked and drank as though he were safe and snug in a tavern back home.

The others renewed their pleas to him to turn back, but the more they begged him

The
Scared Ghost
and
Other
Stories

the more stubborn he became. The wind
snapped the masts in twain as easily as breaking
twigs. The sails were carried away in the fierce
wind. The captain merely laughed and jeered
at his terrified passengers.

Still more violently the storm raged, but the
captain treated with equal contempt the storm's
violence and the fears of his crew and passengers. When his men tried to force him to turn
and take shelter in a bay, he seized the ringlead-
er—the pilot—in his arms and threw him overboard. As he did this, the clouds opened and a
Shape alighted on the quarter deck of the ship.
This Shape may have been the Almighty Himself, or was certainly sent by Him. Crew and
passengers were struck dumb with terror. The
captain, however, went on smoking his pipe
and did not even remove his cap as the Shape
spoke to him.

"Captain," the Shape said, "you are a very
stubborn man."

"And you," cried the captain, "are a rascal!
Who wants a smooth passage? Not I! I want
nothing from you, so clear out and leave me
unless you care to have your brains blown out."

The Shape shrugged his shoulders without
answering.

The captain snatched up a pistol, cocked it,
and pulled the trigger. The bullet, instead of
reaching its target, turned and went through
the captain's hand. At that, his rage knew no

bounds. He leaped up to strike the Shape in the face. But even as he raised his arm it dropped limply at his side. Struggle though he did, the captain could not lift his arm. In helpless anger he cursed and called the Shape all kinds of evil names.

At this the Shape spoke to him.

"From this moment on, you are condemned to sail forever without rest, without anchorage, without reaching any port. You shall never taste beer nor tobacco again. Your drink will be bitter gall; your meat will be red-hot iron. Only a cabin boy will remain, of all this crew. Horns will grow from his forehead and he will have a tiger's face and skin tougher than a dogfish's. It will always be your watch and you will never be able to sleep. The moment you close your eyes a sword will pierce your body. And since you delight in tormenting sailors, you shall torment them forevermore. You shall be the evil spirit of the sea. You will travel all oceans and all latitudes without stopping or resting, and your ship will bring misfortune to all who sight it."

"Amen to that!" the captain cried and laughed.

"And on Judgment Day, Satan will claim you for his own."

"A fig for Satan!" the captain answered.

The Shape vanished. The Dutchman found himself alone with his cabin boy, who had already changed to the evil appearance that had been foretold. All the rest—passengers and crew—had vanished.

From that day the Flying Dutchman has sailed the seas, and he takes pleasure in tricking unlucky mariners. He sets their ships on false courses, leads them onto uncharted shoals, and shipwrecks them. He turns their wine sour and changes all their food into beans. Sometimes he will pretend to be an ordinary ship and send letters on board other ships he meets at sea. If the other captain is so unfortunate as to try to read them, he is lost.

At other times an empty boat will draw along-side the Phantom Ship, a sure omen of bad luck to come. The Flying Dutchman can change the appearance of his ship at will, so that he cannot be recognized, and through the years he has collected around him a new crew. Every one of them comes from the worst criminals, pirates, and bullies of the world's oceans, and every one of them is as cursed and doomed as he.

The Phantom Ship

by Captain Frederick Marryat

The ship had reached the southern coast of Africa sailing on a light and steady breeze when suddenly a bank of clouds rolled up from the east and covered the sky. All was a deep unnatural gloom. The sun, filtering through the clouds, caused an eerie red glow, as though the world burned with fire. The wind that had filled the sails and pushed the ship through the water died, and the sails hung limp. The vessel sat becalmed on a quiet sea, unable to move until the wind returned.

The crew crowded the deck, staring with amazement at the strange sky, and talking about the sudden stillness.

"There—there!" shouted the pilot—a man named Schriften.

Every eye looked. Slowly rising out of the water was the tapering masthead and spars of another vessel. It rose and rose from the watery depths with sails set. Topmasts and topsail yards, lower masts and rigging, the wooden hull, the ports with cannons, and finally the whole of it was above water.

"I have known ships to go *down*," exclaimed the captain, "but never to come *up*."

The Scared Ghost and Other Stories

"It's the Phantom Ship," the pilot screamed, "the Flying Dutchman." Schriften turned to a crewman standing nearby. "There, Philip Vanderdecken, is your ghostly father!"

Philip paid no heed. Standing at the rail, touching the sacred object hidden beneath his shirt, he was deep in thought. "Is it possible," he wondered, "that my search is over?" He saw that sailors on the mysterious vessel were lowering a boat. It disappeared into the fog hovering above the waves.

The captain was by temperament an easily excitable man. The idea that a ghost ship, the Flying Dutchman, was so near set him trembling. "What can we do?" he moaned.

A splash of oars was heard alongside, and a voice called out from the gloom. "I say, my good people, give me a rope to come aboard. I have letters to give you."

No one answered. No one moved to obey.

Schriften rushed to the captain. "Don't take their letters. It means doom. I guarantee it."

A ghost suddenly appeared on the deck. His weather-beaten clothes, fur hat and canvas pants were worn and in need of repair. He held letters in his hand. "Where is the captain?" he asked.

"What do you want?" The captain's quivering voice was only slightly above a whisper.

"Yes—what do you want?" Schriften added loudly.

The Phantom Ship

"What? Are you here, shipmate?" the ghost looked at Schriften. "I thought you had gone to Davy Jones' Locker—drowned long ago."

Laughter was Schriften's answer. A thin, piercing howl of a laugh that jangled the nerves.

The ghost turned to the captain. "The fact, sir, is that we have had bad weather and are off our course. We will be long at sea and wish to send letters home."

"I can't take them," the captain answered. "I'm sorry."

"Can't take them! Well, it's very odd, but every ship refuses our letters. It is very unkind. Seamen should have feeling for brother seamen, especially in distress. It would be a comfort to our wives and families if they could only hear from us."

"I cannot take your letters," replied the captain, growing bolder, "and that's final."

"Let me see your letters," interrupted Philip.

"They must not be touched!" the pilot screamed.

"Out of my way monster!" Philip's tone was menacing. "Don't you dare try to stop me."

"Doomed—doomed—doomed!" The pilot jumped up and down on the deck, then broke into a wild fit of laughter.

"Please don't touch the letters," the captain begged.

Philip held out his hand for the letters.

"Here is one from our second mate to his wife in Amsterdam. She lives on Waser Quay."

"Waser Quay has long been gone, my good friend," replied Philip. "There is now a large dock for ships where it once stood."

"Impossible!" replied the seaman. "Here is another from myself to my sweetheart, Vrow Ketser—with money for her to buy a new brooch."

Philip shook his head. "I remember seeing an old lady of that name buried some thirty years ago."

"How is that? I left her young and blooming Here's one for the house of Slutz and Company, that owns the ship."

"There is no such house now, but I have heard that many years ago there was a firm of that name."

"You must be making a joke with me! Here is a letter from our captain to his son . . ."

Philip seized the letter, but before he could break the seal, Schriften snatched it from his hand and threw it overboard into the sea.

Philip's eyes blazed anger. "That was a scurvy trick, mate."

Schriften didn't answer, but quickly snatched the other letters from the ghost and hurled them after the first.

The ghostly seaman walked to the railing, grief mirrored on his face, and watched until the last of the wet papers sank into the sea.

"That was very hard, very unkind," he wept. "The time may come when you may wish your family to know your situation." So saying, he disappeared.

"What is to be done?" the frightened captain muttered. "What will become of us? I don't know what to do."

"I'll tell you," said Schriften. "That man there, Philip, has a charm hung around his neck. Take it from him, throw it overboard, and your ship will be saved. If you don't, this vessel will be lost—and every soul on board with it."

"Yes, yes, that's right. Depend upon it," cried the sailors. "He speaks the truth!"

"Fools!" Philip yelled, "didn't you hear the ghost call Schriften shipmate. He is the one who will doom us all."

"Yes, yes," cried the sailors, "That's right. The ghost did call him shipmate."

"I tell you Philip is the man. If you value your lives, force him to give up the charm," said Schriften.

"Give up the charm, give up the charm," the sailors chanted.

"Wait! Wait!" he cried. The captain waved his arms to demand silence.

Still, the seamen screamed their confusion. Some were for throwing Schriften overboard, the other side was for tossing Philip into the sea. At last the captain's voice was heard above the

din. He satisfied both sides by ordering Philip
and Schriften overboard into a lifeboat.

The huge hull of the ship towered about the
lifeboat. Only the voices of the crew pierced the
fog—cheers of relief that the ship had been
saved.

Philip rowed away toward the Phantom Ship.
But it appeared to get farther away no matter
how hard he pulled.

"Why don't you throw me overboard?"
Schriften taunted. "Then you will be lighter
and could row faster."

"I felt like throwing you overboard when you
tried to part me from my relic."

"Yes, and I have tried to make others take it
from you this very day. Have I not?"

"You have indeed. Even so, I will not harm
you."

"Do you mean you *forgive* your enemy?"
asked Schriften, doubtfully.

"I do with all my heart."

"Then you have won me to your side." The
pilot's mournful voice sounded above the
splash of the oars. "Your father murdered
me—threw me into the sea to drown. He was
given one chance for his doom to be canceled.
The bargain was that so long as his son and I
remained enemies he would be doomed to sail
without rest, causing harm to all men of the sea.

As Schriften spoke he held out his hand to

Philip in friendship. When Philip grasped it the pilot vanished. He was alone in the boat.

Philip rowed toward the Phantom Ship. The vessel no longer seemed to sail away. Quite the opposite, every pull of the oars brought him nearer and nearer as though the ship waited for him.

"Your captain, I must speak with your captain." Philip addressed a man who appeared to be the first mate.

"Who shall I say wants him?"

"Who?" replied Philip. "Tell him his son would speak with him, his son Philip Vanderdecken."

Shouts of laughter from the crew followed his answer.

"Tell him his son, please," urged Philip.

"Well, sir, here he is coming now," replied the mate, stepping aside and pointing to the captain. "Tell him yourself."

"What is all this?"

"Are you the captain of this vessel?"

"I am, sir."

"And who are you?" the puzzled captain asked.

"Time has stopped with you, but with those who live in the world, it stops not. In me behold your son, Philip." As Philip spoke, he removed the golden chain hung around his neck and held the relic out to his father. "Your wandering, dear father, is over."

As the captain took the cross the long tapering upper spars of the ghost ship, the yards and sails fell into dust, fluttered in the air, and sank upon the waves. The mainmast, foremast, bowsprit, everything above the deck crumbled and disappeared. The heavy iron guns crashed through the decks and splashed into the water. The crew crumbled down into skeletons, dust, and fragments of ragged garments. The beam and timbers separated, the decks of the vessel slowly sank, and the remnants of the hull floated upon the water. At last the ghostly father disappeared beneath the deep blue waves. The Phantom Ship was gone forever.

Philip swam to his lifeboat and climbed aboard. Then did the clouds in the sky roll away swift as thought. The sun again burst out in all its splendor. The screaming seagulls again whirled in the air. Porpoises tumbled and tossed in play, and dolphins leaped from the sparkling sea.

The Faithful Ghost

by Jerome K. Jerome

I was very young when I first met Johnson. I was home from boarding school for the Christmas holidays. In fact it was the first Christmas we spent in the new house my parents had bought. I remember it was around midnight on Christmas Eve that I first saw him. I got out of bed to go downstairs, and had just opened my bedroom door when I found myself face to face with Johnson. He passed right through me, and uttering a long low wail of misery, disappeared out the window.

I was startled for the moment. I had never seen a ghost before, and I felt nervous about turning out the light and going to bed. So I tiptoed to my father's room to tell him what I had seen. "Oh yes, that was old Johnson," he answered. "Don't be afraid of him. He lived here." And then he told me the history of Johnson's ghost.

It seemed that when Johnson was alive, he had loved a girl who lived in our house. She was a beautiful girl named Emily. Johnson was quite young then and too poor to marry her. So he kissed her goodbye and told her he would return as soon as he made his fortune.

Johnson went off to find gold in Australia, which was what English people did in those days if they wanted to get rich quick. As it happened, Johnson didn't labor in the mines digging gold, he stole it—and many other things too. He robbed all the travelers he could find. Of course, in those days travelers through the bush were few and far between, so it took Johnson nearly twenty years to make his fortune. At last, however, when he thought he had enough he escaped the law, and returned to England to claim his bride.

He reached the house, only to find it silent and deserted. All the neighbors could tell him was that Emily's family had moved away. Nobody had seen or heard anything of them since they left.

Johnson searched all over the world for his lost love, but he never found her. After years of wasted effort, he returned to spend his last years in the house where he and his Emily had passed so many happy hours.

He lived there all alone, wandering about the empty rooms, weeping and calling to his Emily to come back to him. And when the old fellow died, his ghost kept on weeping and wailing, too. (Although, as far as we know, he never shed a tear over his wicked deeds in Australia.)

My father told me that Johnson's ghost was there when they first took the house. In fact, the agent had lowered the rent because the place was haunted.

Well, after that, we were continually meeting

Johnson about the house. At first we used to walk around him or stand aside to let him pass. But as we grew more used to having the ghost around, there seemed no need to be so formal, and we would just walk right through him.

Whatever he had done during his lifetime, Johnson's ghost was gentle and harmless, and we all felt sorry for him. In fact, the women made quite a pet of him—for a while. His faithfulness to his lost Emily touched them so.

But as time went on, my parents grew tired of Johnson. You see, the ghost was full of sadness. There was nothing cheerful about him. He would sit on the stairs and cry for hours at a time. And when we had a party, the ghost would come and sob outside the living-room door. His weeping cast such a gloom over everybody that our parties weren't much fun at all. After a while we could hardly get guests to come to our house.

"I'm getting sick and tired of this," said Father one evening. (Johnson had just spoiled a good game of chess for him by moaning and groaning until my father couldn't tell his king from the pawns.) "We'll have to get rid of him somehow."

"Well," said my mother, "you'll never see the last of him until he's found his Emily's grave. That's what he's after. You find Emily's grave for him, and he'll stay there. That's the only thing to do."

It seemed like a good idea, but the trouble

was that nobody knew where to find Emily's grave. My father suggested that we could show some other Emily's grave to the old robber. But as luck would have it, there wasn't a single Emily buried anywhere for miles around. In fact, you never came across a neighborhood so completely without an Emily as ours was.

I felt sorry for the old ghost, and wanted to see him happy after all these years, so I offered a suggestion. "Couldn't we make a grave for old Johnson?" I asked. "We could try it, anyway."

"Excellent!" exclaimed my father. "We'll do just that!"

The very next morning we had the gardener fix up a little mound at the bottom of the orchard with a tombstone over it bearing the following inscription:

SACRED

To the memory of

EMILY

Her Last Words Were:

"Tell Johnson I Love Him."

"That ought to do it!" said my father. "I certainly hope it does."

I hoped so, too. Johnson's sadness was beginning to affect me. I felt guilty every time I laughed.

The Faithful Ghost

We led the ghost down to the "newly discovered grave" that very night. And well, it was one of the most pathetic things I've ever seen—the way Johnson took on at the sight of that tombstone. He wept and wept so much that Dad and the gardener cried like children when they saw him take on so.

Johnson's ghost has never troubled us since then. He spends every night sobbing by the grave, and he seems quite content.

Oh yes! In case you want to visit him, he is generally there 10 p.m. to 4 a.m.—10 to 2 on Saturdays.

The Boarded Window

by Ambrose Bierce

retold

The man's name was said to be Murlock. He looked about seventy years old, although actually he was only about fifty. Something besides years had a hand in his aging. His hair and long full beard were white, his dull gray eyes sunken, his face seamed and wrinkled. He was tall and spare with a stoop of the shoulders. I never saw him; these particulars I learned from my grandfather, from whom I also got this story when I was a lad.

One day Murlock was found in his cabin, dead. It was not a time and a place for coroners and newspapers, being 1830 and a few miles outside of Cincinnati in the wilderness. I suppose it was agreed that he had died from natural causes, because if I had been told differently, I would remember. I only know that the body was buried near the cabin, alongside the grave of his wife. She had died so many years earlier that not many local folks remembered her —even though her ghost was said to haunt the spot.

When Murlock built his cabin he was young, strong, and full of hope. Back east, he had married a devoted young woman who came to the wilderness to share the dangers and hardships of life. There is no known record of her name; of her charms of mind and person tradition is silent. But of the love Murlock felt for her there is little doubt. For what else but the memory of her could have chained him to a crumbling cabin in the woods for so many years?

As my grandfather told the story, Murlock returned from hunting in a distant part of the forest to find his wife near death from fever. There was no physician within miles, no neighbor; nor was she in any condition to be left while he went for help. So he set about the task of nursing her back to health. But by the end of the third day she fell into unconsciousness and passed away.

When convinced that she was dead, Murlock prepared her for burial. In performance of this sacred duty he blundered now and again, did certain things wrong, and others which he did correctly were done over and over. His occasional failures to perform some simple and ordinary act filled him with astonishment like that of a drunken man who wonders at the suspension of natural laws that makes him fall when he should stand. He was surprised, too, that he did not weep—surprised and a little ashamed. Surely it was unkind not to weep for the dead.

"Tomorrow," he said aloud, "I shall have to make the coffin and dig the grave. And then I shall miss her, when she is no longer in sight. But now—she is dead."

He stood over the body in the fading light, adjusting the hair and putting the finishing touches to the simple toilet. He completed his work and sank into a chair by the side of the table where the body lay.

At that moment came in through the open window a long, wailing sound like the cry of a lost child in the far deep of the darkening wood! But the man did not move. Again, and nearer than before, sounded that unearthly cry. Perhaps it was a wild beast; perhaps it was a dream, for Murlock was asleep.

Some hours later, as it afterward appeared, he awoke—he knew not why. There in the darkness by the side of the dead, he strained his eyes to see—he knew not what. His senses were all alert, his breath was stopped. His blood had stilled its tides as if to assist the silence. Who— what had waked him, and where was it?

Suddenly the table shook, and at the same moment he heard, or fancied that he heard, a light, soft step—another—sounds as of bare feet upon the floor!

He was terrified beyond the power to cry out or move. He waited—waited there in the darkness through seeming centuries of the worst dread that one might know, yet live to tell. He tried vainly to speak the dead woman's name, vainly to stretch forth his hand across the table to learn if she were there. His throat was power-less, his arms and hands were like lead.

Then something most frightening happened. A heavy object was thrown against the table with such force that the table was pushed against his chest so hard he almost fell over. He heard and felt the fall of something upon the floor with such an impact that the whole cabin shook. There was the noise of scuffling and a confusion of sounds impossible to describe. He flung his hands upon the table. Nothing was there!

Murlock sprang to the wall, with a little grop-ing seized his loaded rifle, and without aim fired. By the flash which lit up the room, he saw an enormous panther dragging the dead wom-an toward the window, its teeth fixed in her throat! Then there was darkness blacker than before, and silence. When he returned to con-sciousness the sun was high and the wood vocal with songs of birds.

The body lay near the window, where the beast had left it when frightened away by the flash and noise of the rifle. The clothing was torn and the long hair in disorder. The ribbon with which he had bound the wrists was broken. The hands were tightly clenched into fists. Between the teeth was a fragment of the ani-mal's ear.

The Phantom Coach

by Amelia B. Edwards

The day dawned crisp and cold as December mornings in the north of England are apt to. The grouse-hunting season was nearly over; still I shouldered my gun and set out to try my luck. Sunset found me with two birds in my bag and no notion at all of where I was—except that it was somewhere on a bleak, wide moor. Not the faintest smoke wreath, not the tiniest cultivated patch, or fence, or sheep track met my eyes in any direction. I was lost. Through the gathering darkness I could see a range of low hills some ten or twelve miles distant. There was nothing to do but walk in that direction and take my chance on finding help.

I had gone barely a mile before weariness overtook me. Under ordinary circumstances a ten-mile walk would have been easy, but I had been on foot since an hour after daybreak and had not eaten since breakfast. Tiredness and hunger, however, were the least of my worries. For as the darkness of evening closed in, the first feathery flakes of a snowstorm floated silently to the ground.

I began to remember stories of weary travelers who lay down to rest and were

The Scared Ghost and Other Stories

gently covered over with a smothering cold blanket of snow. Death! I shuddered at the thought and walked faster. I stopped and shouted every now and then, but my cries seemed to make the silence deeper. A vague sense of uneasiness settled upon me. I shouted again, louder this time, and listened eagerly. As night came on the cold grew more intense. Snow crunched under foot. Was my call answered? Or did I fancy hearing a far-off cry? I shouted. An echo—or was it an answer? A wavering speck of light came suddenly out of the darkness, shifting, growing momentarily brighter. I ran toward it at full speed and found myself—to my great joy—face to face with an old man carrying a lantern.

"Thank God!" burst from my lips.

Blinking and frowning, he peered into my face. "What for?"

"Well—for you," I stammered. "I was lost in the snow."

"If the Lord had a mind for you to be lost"—his voice was flat and toneless—"then lost you'd be."

"I would give ten guineas for a guide and a horse to get me to Dowling," I said hopefully.

"The mail coach from the north passes about five miles over there." He pointed toward the horizon. "Seeing as how the weather is so bad, you can probably get a ride in it."

He held the lantern high and walked away, then stopped and looked back over his shoulder at me. I had known a good hunting dog once that made the same gesture when it wanted to be followed. I hurried after the old man.

Presently—at the end, as it seemed to me, of only a few minutes—he came to a sudden halt.

"Yon's your road. Keep the stone fence to your right hand and you can't fail the way. At the crossroad you can wave the mail coach to stop."

"How far before I get there?"

"Nigh upon three miles, I guess. It won't take long. This is a fair road for walking, but it's a might too steep and narrow for the coach traffic from the north—but that don't stop them from using it. Be careful down near the crossroad signpost where the guard rail is broken 'way. It's not been mended since the accident."

"What accident?"

"The night mail coach broke through the rail and pitched right over into the valley, a good fifty feet down. The rescuers found four dead. The other two died the next morning."

It seemed to me he talked too easily of death, almost as if telling me what he had eaten for lunch.

". . . Happened just about nine years ago," he continued.

I opened my purse and handed him a half crown. I had had enough talk of horror.

"Near the signpost, you say? I will remember to be careful."

"Good night, sir, and thankee." He pocketed

the coin, made faint pretense of touching his hat, and trudged back the way he had come.

I watched the light of his lantern till it disappeared, then turned to go my way alone. Despite the dead darkness overhead, the line of the stone fence showed clearly against the pale gleam of the snow. How silent it seemed with only my footsteps to listen to! I hummed a tune to chase away shadows lurking by the side of the road.

The night air seemed to become colder and colder. Though I walked fast I found it impossible to keep warm. I lost sensation in my hands, and grasped my gun with numb fingers. My feet were like ice. I even breathed with difficulty as though climbing a great hill instead of crossing a quiet north-country road. Every few minutes I had to stop and lean against the stone fence to catch my breath.

After about a mile, I stood beside the fence gasping for breath. I glanced over my shoulder down the road I had walked. A gleaming point of light, like the lantern the old man carried flickered against the blackness. At first I thought that it was he—following me. Even as the thought occurred to me, a second light flashed into sight, parallel with the first like gleaming yellow eyes. I knew they had to be carriage lamps.

The lamps grew larger and brighter every moment. The vehicle was coming on fast and noiselessly as the snow was now nearly a foot deep. A sudden suspicion dawned upon me. Was it possible that I had passed the cross-road in the dark without noticing the signpost? Could this be the mail coach?

I jumped forward, waving my hat and shouting. The coach came on at full speed. Four huge gray horses kicked up snow as they passed me. For a moment I feared that I had not been seen or heard, but it was only a moment. The driver pulled up. The guard—muffled to the eyes in capes and comforters against the cold—made no move to dismount to help me on board. I opened the door myself and climbed inside with the other passengers.

The atmosphere of the coach seemed, if possible, colder than outdoors. Worse than the cold, however, was an oddly disagreeable smell that hovered overall.

"How intensely cold it is tonight." I addressed the man sitting across from me.

He lifted his head, looked at me, but made no comment.

"The winter," I added, "seems to have begun in earnest."

Although the corner in which he sat was so dim that I could not see his features, I knew that his eyes were turned full upon me. Yet he answered not a word.

At any other time I would have felt annoyed, and probably would have told the man that he was rude. At the moment, though, I felt too sick to protest. The icy coldness of the night air had struck a chill to the very marrow of my bones, and the smell inside the coach had made me sick to my stomach. I hoped I wouldn't vomit. I turned to the man sitting beside me and asked if he would object to my opening the window.

He neither spoke nor stirred. I repeated the question, but with the same result. If the man was bothered by the breeze, too bad! I reached for the sash to open the window. As I pulled, the leather strap broke in my hand.

"What the devil . . ." I muttered.

Before I could get further in my complaint, I noticed that the window was covered with a thick coat of mildew, such as would take years to accumulate. Surprised, I turned my full attention to the coach. Every part of it was decaying. The sashes splintered at a touch. The leather fittings were crusted over with mold. The floor was almost rotting away beneath my feet.

Suddenly the fine hair on my neck tingled as though many-legged spiders crawled over me. I slowly turned my eyes from the coach to the passengers. As long as I live I shall never forget their bloodless lips drawn back in the agony of death. These were not living men. Decay played upon their awful faces; upon their hair, dank with the dews of the grave; upon their clothes, earth-stained and dropping into pieces; upon their hands, which were the hands of corpses long buried. Only their eyes, their terrible eyes, were living.

A wild cry for help and mercy tore from my lips as I flung myself against the door and struggled to open it. Through the window the frozen countryside rushed by. As in a dream, I saw the ghastly signpost rearing its warning finger. The coach reeled like a ship at sea . . . the broken railing . . . the black gulf below . . . the crash . . . crushing pain—and blackness.

It seemed as if years had gone by when I awoke one morning from a deep sleep and found my wife watching by my bedside. I will give, in half a dozen words, the tale she told me with tears of thanksgiving. I had fallen over a precipice near the junction of the old coach road and the new, and had only been saved from certain death by landing on a deep snowdrift. I was discovered at daybreak by shepherds who carried me to the nearest house and brought a doctor to tend me. He set my broken arm, and confined me to bed because of a compound fracture of the skull. Papers in my pocket showed my address, and my wife was summoned.

The place of my fall, you may have guessed, was the exact spot of the frightful accident of the north mail coach nine years earlier.

The Signalman

by Charles Dickens

retold

"Hello! Below there!"

When he heard a voice thus calling to him, he was standing at the door of his hut, with a flag in his hand, furled around its short pole. Considering that he was standing near enough to me, one would have thought he would have known immediately from which direction the call had come. But instead of looking up to where I stood on the top of a steep overhanging cliff, he looked down the railroad line.

"Hello! Below!" I called again.

From looking down the tracks, he turned and saw me.

"Is there any path by which I can come down and speak to you?"

He looked up at me without replying.

I repeated my question. After a long pause, during which he seemed to examine me very carefully, he motioned with his rolled-up flag toward a point some two or three hundred yards distant. I made for the point, and found a rough, extremely steep path, which I followed.

When I came down low enough upon the zigzag descent to see him again, he was standing between the rails. His pose suggested that he was waiting for me to appear. There was such watchfulness in his attitude that I stopped for a moment, wondering at it.

Stepping out upon the level of the railroad and drawing nearer to him, I saw that he was a dark, sallow man, with a dark beard and rather heavy eyebrows.

His post was as solitary and dismal a place as ever I saw. On either side, a dripping-wet wall of jagged stone. In the other direction, a gloomy red light and the even gloomier entrance to a black tunnel. So little sunlight found its way to this spot that it had an unearthly, deadly smell. So much cold wind rushed through that it struck a chill to me, as if I had left the natural world.

This was a lonesome post to have, I said to him. It caught my attention as I looked down from up there.

He directed a most curious look toward the red light near the tunnel's mouth. He looked all about it as if something were missing from it, and then looked at me.

"That light is part of your job?" I asked.

He answered in a low voice, "Don't you know it is?"

The monstrous thought came into my mind as I gazed into the bright eyes under his hairy brows—this is a spirit, not a living man! I stepped back. But in making the sudden motion, I noticed that the look in his eyes was fear of *me*.

"You look at me," I said, forcing a smile, "as if you had a dread of me."

"I was wondering," he answered, "whether I had seen you before."

"Where?"

He pointed to the red light he had looked at earlier.

"There?" I said.

"Yes." He nodded.

"My good fellow, what should I do there?"

His manner cleared—mine too.

He took me into his hut, where there was a fire, a desk for an official book in which he had to make certain entries, a telegraphic instrument with its dial face and needles, and a little bell.

We sat by the fire and talked. He readily answered my questions. In his lonely spot he had taught himself a language. He had also worked at fractions and decimals, and had tried a little algebra. But he was, he said, a poor hand at figures.

He was several times interrupted by the little bell, and had to read messages and send replies. Once, he had to stand outside and display the flag as a train passed. He was most exact in his duties and would stop in the middle of a syllable to do a chore. In a word, I should have set this man down as one of the safest of men to be employed as a signalman. Yet, twice as he was speaking to me he broke off and turned his face toward the bell when it did *not* ring. And each time the color drained from his face. And each time he opened the door of the hut (which was kept shut to keep out the unearthly damp), and looked out toward the red light near the mouth of the tunnel. On both of those occasions he came back to the fire with an uneasy air upon him.

When I rose to leave him, I said, "You almost make me think that I have met a contented man."

(I must confess I said that to lead him on to talk about what was worrying him.)

"I believe I used to be," he answered in a low voice, "but I am troubled, sir, I am troubled."

"With what? What is your trouble?"

"It is very, very difficult for me to speak of. If you ever make me another visit, I will try to tell you."

"But I do intend to come again. Say when shall it be?"

"I go off early in the morning, and I shall be on again at ten tomorrow night, sir."

"I will come at eleven."

He thanked me, and went out at the door with me. "I'll show my white light, sir," he said in his strange low voice, "'till you have found the way up. When you have found it, don't call out! And when you are at the top, don't call out!"

His manner seemed to make the place strike colder to me, but I said no more than "Very well."

"And when you come down tomorrow night, don't call out! Let me ask you a parting question. What made you cry, 'Hello! Below there!' tonight?"

"Heaven knows," said I. "I cried something to that effect—"

"Not to that effect, sir. Those were the very words. I know them well."

"I said them, no doubt, because I saw you below."

"For no other reason?"

"What other reason could I possibly have?"

"You had no feeling that they were told to you in a supernatural way?"

"No."

He wished me good night, and held up his light. I walked by the side of the rails (with the very disagreeable feeling of a train coming behind me), until I found the path. It was easier to climb up than to come down, and I got back to my inn without any adventure.

The next night, I placed my foot on the path down to his hut as the distant clocks were striking eleven. He was waiting for me at the bottom, with his white light on.

"I have not called out," I said, when we came close together. "May I speak now?"

"By all means, sir."

"Good night, then, and here's my hand."

"Good night, sir, and here's mine."

His handshake was firm. With that, we walked side by side to his hut, entered it, closed the door, and sat down by the fire.

"I have made up my mind, sir," he began, bending forward as soon as we were seated, and speaking in a tone but a little above a whisper, "that you shall not have to ask me twice what troubles me. I took you for someone else yesterday evening. That troubles me."

"Who is it?"

"I don't know. I never saw the face. The left arm is across the face, and the right arm is waved. Violently waved. This way."

I followed his action with my eyes, and it was the action of an arm signaling with the utmost passion: *For God's sake clear the way!*

"One moonlight night," said the man, "I was sitting here, when I heard a voice cry, 'Hello! Below there!' I started up, looked from that door, and saw this someone standing by the red light near the tunnel, waving as I just now showed you. The voice seemed hoarse with shouting, and it cried, 'Look out! Look out!' And then again, 'Hello! Below there! Look out!' I grabbed my lamp, turned it on red, and ran toward the figure, calling, 'What's wrong?'

What has happened? Where?' It stood just outside the blackness of the tunnel. I came so close upon it that I wondered at its keeping the sleeve across its eyes. I ran right up at it, and had my hand stretched out to pull the sleeve away, when it was gone."

"Into the tunnel," said I.

"No, I ran on into the tunnel, five hundred yards. I stopped and held my lamp above my head—nothing. I ran back here and telegraphed both ways: *An alarm has been given. Is anything wrong?* The answer came back, both ways: *All well.*"

Touching my arm, he slowly added these words—

"Within six hours after the ghost, a terrible accident happened on this line, and within ten hours the dead and wounded were brought along through the tunnel over the spot where the figure had stood."

A disagreeable shudder crept over me, but I did my best against it. "A remarkable coincidence," I said. He said he was not finished.

"This," he said, again laying his hand upon my arm, and glancing over his shoulder with hollow eyes, "was just a year ago. Six or seven months passed, and I had recovered from the surprise and shock, when one morning, as the day was breaking, I—standing at that door—looked toward the red light and saw the specter again."

"Did it cry out?"

"No. It was silent."

"Did it wave its arm?"

"No, it stood with both hands before the face. Like this."

Once more I followed his action with my eyes. It was an action of mourning. I have seen such a pose in stone figures on tombs. "Did you go up to it?"

"I came in and sat down, partly to collect my thoughts, partly because seeing it again made me faint. When I went to the door again, the ghost was gone."

"But nothing followed? Nothing came of this?"

He touched me on the arm with his forefinger twice, giving a ghastly nod each time.

"That very day, as a train came out of the tunnel I noticed, at a carriage window on my side, what looked like a confusion of hands, and something waved. I saw it, just in time to signal the driver, Stop! He shut off, and put his brake on, but the train drifted past here a hundred and fifty yards or more. I ran after it, and heard terrible screams and cries. A beautiful young lady had just died instantly—dropped dead. She was brought in here and laid down on this floor."

I pushed my chair back, as I looked from the boards at which he pointed, to himself.

"True, sir, true. I tell you exactly as it happened."

My mouth was very dry, and I could think of nothing to say. Outside, the wind seemed to take up the story with a long lamenting wail.

He continued. "Now, sir, mark this, and judge how my mind is troubled. The specter came back, a week ago. Ever since, it has been there, off and on."

"At the light?"

"At the danger light."

"What does it seem to do?"

He repeated, if possible with increased passion, that former signal—*For God's sake clear the way!*

Then he went on. "I have no peace or rest from it. It calls to me for minutes at a time, 'Below there! Look out! Look out!' It stands waving to me. It rings my little bell—"

I seized on that point. "Did it ring your bell yesterday evening when I was here, and you went to the door?"

"Twice it rang the bell."

"Your imagination misleads you!" I exclaimed. "For my eyes were on the bell, and my ears were open to the bell, and if I am a living man, it did not ring at those times. No, nor at any other time, except when it was rung in the natural course of physical things by the station communicating with you."

He shook his head. "I have never made a
mistake as to that, yet, sir. I have never con-
fused the specter's ring with a living man's. The
ghost's ring is a strange vibration in the bell that
is not there when a man rings. I don't wonder
that you failed to hear it. But *I* heard it."

"And did the specter seem to be there, when
you looked out?"

"It *was* there!"

"Both times?"

He repeated firmly, "Both times."

"Will you come to the door and look for it
now?" I asked.

He bit his lower lip as though unwilling, but
rose. I opened the door, and stood on the step
while he stood in the doorway. There was the
danger light. There was the dismal mouth of
the tunnel. There were the high, wet, stone
walls of the cliff. There were the stars above
them.

"Do you see it?" I asked him.

"No," he answered. "It is not there."

"Agreed," said I.

We went in again, shut the door, and sat
down.

"By this time you will fully understand, sir,
that what troubles me so dreadfully is the question, what does the ghost mean?"

I was not sure, I told him.

"If I telegraph *Danger* on either side of me,
or on both, I can give no reason for it. I should

get into trouble and do no good. They would think I was mad. This is the way it would work. Message: *Danger, take care!* Answer: *What danger? Where?* Message: *Don't know. But for God's sake take care!* They would replace me. What else could they do?"

When I left him that night, he was in a most depressed state of mind from his cruel haunting. I had offered to stay the night, but he would not hear of it.

Next evening was lovely and I walked out early to enjoy it before time to go down to the signalman's hut. Still, something drew me to the cliff to take a quick look down before I began my stroll. I stepped to the brink and looked down to the point where I had first seen him. I cannot describe the thrill that seized upon me when, close to the mouth of the tunnel, I saw the appearance of a man, with his left sleeve across his eyes, passionately waving his right arm.

The nameless horror that oppressed me passed in a moment, for I saw that the man was waving to a little group of men standing at a short distance. The danger light was off.

With a sense that something was wrong, I raced down the path.

"What's the matter?" I asked the men.

"The signalman was killed this morning, sir."

"Not the man belonging to that hut?"

"Yes, sir."

"Not the man I know?"

"You will recognize him, sir, if you knew him," said the man who spoke for the others as he raised the canvas covering a body.

It was indeed the signalman.

The man who had stood waving at the mouth of the tunnel walked up. He was the train driver.

"I called to him as loud as I could, sir," he addressed me.

"What did you say?"

"I said, 'Below there! Look out! Look out! For God's sake clear the way!' I put my left arm up before my eyes, not to see, and I waved this right arm to the last—but it was no use."

The Wind in the Rosebush

by Mary Wilkins Freeman

"You must be Rebecca!" John Dent's widow smiled. "Your letter arrived only this morning."

"I didn't think you would get it, but I hope you don't mind my coming anyway," Rebecca apologized. "I just couldn't wait to see Agnes!"

"It's no trouble at all, my dear. But please come inside."

Rebecca picked up her small suitcase and had set one foot over the doorsill when a sudden motion near the flagstone terrace caught her eye. A rosebush shook violently as though brushed by a sudden gust of wind. Yet not a leaf trembled on the plants growing nearby.

"Will you look at that!" she exclaimed.

Mrs. Dent poked her head out the door to get a better view. "I don't see anything."

"That rosebush—it was moving!"

"Well, it isn't now," said Mrs. Dent. "But it is a little cool standing out here. Come inside."

The house was not as Rebecca remembered it when her sister, the first Mrs. Dent, was alive. "You have all new furniture," she remarked, and noted that Mrs. Dent had expensive tastes—Brussels carpets, lace curtains, brilliant upholstery, and polished wood.

"I never was one to want dead folks' things. I had your sister's old furniture put up at auction."

Rebecca fought to control her anger. She could just imagine strangers rummaging through her sister's belongings.

"I hope you saved something for Agnes. When she's grown up, she will want some of her mother's things."

"There's stuff left in the attic. Agnes can have it."

Rebecca knew that she and the woman wouldn't get along. Something in the icy eyes, yes that was it—icy. The woman was cold and unfeeling, probably cruel, too.

"Where is my niece?" Rebecca looked out the window; it would be dark soon. "Isn't it time she was at home?"

"When she gets over to Addie Slocum's she never knows when to come home."

"Is Addie her best friend?"

"I guess you might say Addie is her best friend. They spend a lot of time together."

Rebecca wanted to know everything about her sister's child. She was sorry to have left the girl with her stepmother so long. It must have been a terrible year for Agnes, especially after her father died.

"Maybe Addie can come out to Michigan to visit when Agnes moves there to live with me— Oh! There she is now." Rebecca caught sight of Agnes through the window.

"She isn't as late as I reckoned she'd be."

Rebecca thought she heard a note of nervousness in the woman's voice, but quickly dismissed the idea. Must be her imagination. Why wouldn't the woman want her to see Agnes?

"Where is she?" Rebecca looked at the door waiting for it to open.

"I guess she stopped to take off her hat in the hallway," Mrs. Dent answered.

Rebecca rushed to the door and looked outside. There was no one there. "Agnes!" she called, "Agnes it's me—Rebecca!" No voice answered.

"You must have made a mistake about seeing her."

Mrs. Dent sounded relieved. Rebecca was certain of it.

"You've been thinking about her so much that you thought you saw her. It was your imagination. I knew it was too early for her to be home from Addie Slocum's."

When Rebecca went to bed Agnes still had not returned. She lay awake for a long time listening to hear her come in. But the train ride had been long—two days—and she was exhausted. She didn't remember falling asleep.

The next morning Rebecca was down early. She found Mrs. Dent in the kitchen preparing breakfast.

"What time did Agnes get home last night?" she asked cheerfully.

"She didn't get home." Mrs. Dent talked while she poured coffee.

"What!"

"She stayed the night at the Slocums'. She often does."

"Without sending you word?"

"She knew I wouldn't worry."

Rebecca tried to hide her concern, for she knew of no good reason for alarm. What was wrong with staying the night at a friend's house? Still, she was worried and had lost her appetite.

"Please excuse me," she apologized. "I'm not hungry."

"You're just overtired," Mrs. Dent diagnosed, "and no wonder too, what with that long train ride from Michigan. You should go back to bed and get more rest."

"Perhaps you're right," Rebecca said weakly. She did feel wrung out.

Rebecca went to her room. Her scream tore through the house. Mrs. Dent met the pale woman rushing down the stairs.

"Agnes's nightgown—on my bed—" she stammered. "Laid out on my bed." She grasped Mrs. Dent firmly by the shoulders. *"Laid out—"*

she yelled, "with arms folded across the bosom and a red rose like it was being held in her dead hands."

The blood seemed to drain from Mrs. Dent's face. Her breath came quickly in short spasms.

"Now, I want to know what all this means," Rebecca demanded.

Mrs. Dent regained control of herself. "What what means?"

"Is this house haunted?" Rebecca demanded, pressing her fingers hard into the woman's soft flesh.

"I don't know anything about a house being haunted. I don't believe in such things." Mrs. Dent spoke with gathering force. The color flashed in her cheeks. "You must be crazy!"

"No," said Rebecca shortly. "I'm not crazy, but I shall be if this keeps up much longer. I'm going to find out where my niece is before night."

Mrs. Dent eyed her coldly. "How?"

"I'm going to the Slocums'."

But Rebecca didn't go to the Slocums'. An urgent cable called her back to Michigan. The wire said that her mother had fallen down the cellar stairs and suffered serious injury. Mrs. Dent promised to send Agnes to Michigan as soon as she could get her ready. Rebecca left money to pay for her train fare.

When Rebecca arrived two days later, she found her mother in perfect health. She knew then that Mrs. Dent had tricked her. She wanted to return immediately, but fatigue and nervous exhaustion had her near physical and mental collapse. The doctor strongly advised against another long train trip.

From her bed Rebecca wrote to Mrs. Dent, but got no answer. She wrote to the Slocums. Nothing was heard. Finally, in desperation, she sent a telegram to the postmaster asking for any information that he could give. His reply was short and to the point.

Madam:

No Slocums in this vicinity. Your niece Agnes disappeared about this time a year ago. Believed dead. Body never found. Whereabouts of Mrs. Dent unknown. House said to be haunted.

Yours truly,

Thomas Amblecrom, postmaster.